This is love: to fly toward a secret sky,
to cause a hundred veils to fall each moment.
First to let go of life.
Finally, to take a step without feet.

~ Rumi

Reflecting the Sky

by

Kaylle Rose

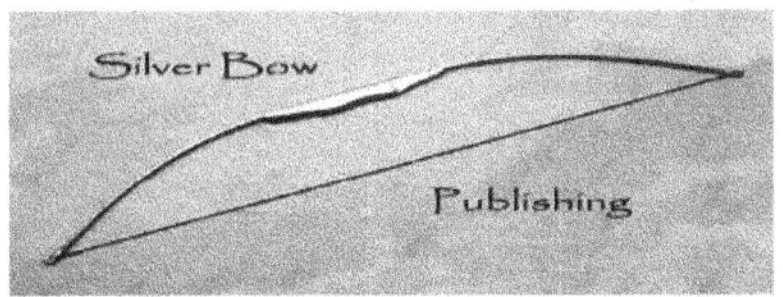

720 – Sixth Street, Box # 5
New Westminster, BC
V3C 3C5   CANADA

Title: Reflecting the Sky
Author: Kaylie Rose
Cover Photo: "Storm Brewing" painting by Candice James
Layout and Design: Candice James
Editor: Candice James

www.silverbowpublishing.com
© Silver Bow Publishing
info@silverbowpublishing.com

ISBN: 9781774032299 book
ISBN: 9781774032305 e book

Library and Archives Canada Cataloguing in Publication

Title: Reflecting the sky / by Kaylie Rose.
Names: Rose, Kaylie, author.
Description: Poems.
Identifiers: Canadiana (print) 20220279306 | Canadiana (ebook) 20220279365 | ISBN 9781774032299 (softcover) | ISBN 9781774032305 (PDF)
Classification: LCC PS3618.0795 R44 2022 | DDC 811/.6—dc23

Dedication

To my biggest fan and sounding board.
Thank you mom.
I love you and miss you so much!

6

Contents

Nigh on a Windy Hill

Nigh on a windy hill, just a stone's throw from my place
A lone tire-swing sways.
Slowly creaks the tired branch that holds the rope,
The rope whose hemp has softened in the sun.
Worn and brittle it frays in the silent air.
It has seen its share of summers,
Been buffered by enough seasons to know their breadth,
To remember childhood laughter now as fading memories ...

The summer days had been golden honey,
Sweeter still than that amber flow,
And the breeze as smooth as silk.
Glazed by the pollen of a thousand stars,
Their fragile petals nestled
Among blades of verdant grass.
The blues, the yellows, the reds
Now faded with the gray of time.

The flutter of a little girl's dress,
Her knees, dimpled knobs, pumping along the eyelet hem,
Her shoes of softened leather, molded and supple
From hours of lazy play.

Pictures in the sky.
Castles made of clouds.
Dreams of butterflies and rainbows.
They were capering ponies
Prancing through our minds;
Wild stallions, neon and strong.
Bigger than the world.
So grand, so consuming, so full of delight and wonder.
The sky swallowed us up like coveted water
And carried us sky-high on bluebird wings.

The sky a dusty copper
Above the melting fire of the sun,
The air tasted like flowers, the grass like heat.
The wood of the fence railings settled

In the last of summer's rays,
Faded and softly aged from long and lazy days.
Piano lessons in the parlor,
The tinkling notes fluttering through opened windows
Brushing back the day's curtains in their satin wake.
My window overlooking the gardens,
The tree line softening the white heat
Of the now departing sun.

The air tastes like smoke as change blows in
With its bristling broom of autumn breeze.
When I look at the clouds now, I swallow the sky.
And somewhere in that lonely, endless space within me
Images of you rise up and I realize
Love was far more complicated
Than my dreams would allow.

And every word was powerless to capture the illusion
That was my awakening,
Nothing will ever again be as simple as those clouds,
Or the dandelion seeds drifting on the wind
Those long-ago summer days.

Tears of Stars

Against this shallow sky, whose depths I cannot perceive,
Stars are tears that infrequently fall
And leave their sparkle in her eyes,
Their glittering tails on her cheeks.
Scandalized by the blackness,
Few people keep their eyes fixed.
Most turn away from
What could swallow them whole.

And in the morning gleams,
Like pearl and golden rivers,
The sunrise those distant tears praise in the dark.
This dim tumult of awesome beauty,
Stark and lovely in its contrast,
Like rocky, divine-worked rock formations
Stained red even in the shade,
And the glistening, diamond dust sands of the sea.
In the black deserts, they find their reflection
Twinkling back beneath the sun
To their sun-dark skies.

She keeps a wary kinship with those celestial tears,
Constant the silent vigil they keep
As the nights fill with weighty moments
And remembered dreams.
Their aroma sweet, like the flower petals,
As they brush inside the window
And caress the gauzy curtains.

Gone are the days past and the days ahead too
When mocked in unfounded hope's cool shadow.
What we want, what we need, what we can believe
Upon waking slips from our grasp
Like fog through our fingers.
The fancies of this beating heart,
Beyond what her hands can touch,
Only in her mind can come to be.

The song of wistfulness
Is a pillow beneath her fragile cheek
When memories repeated chorus
Is pleasant and precious, only returnable in sleep.
Drops of regret like rain in the sunlight,
A thick screen of prismatic color
To flavor memories' warm touch,
But ill-suited to beat the dust,
And make remorse rise in clouds.
This swirling tempest to barrage the mind.
Make no thought quiet.
Bitter mingled with the sweet,
The company of angels, be they black or white,
Roaring in her soul.

Pausing to make room for the reflective eye,
Hands pressed against the wooden sill,
Head bowed, mind consumed with dizzying scope
Of nightmare and reality.

The solid, soft grain of the wood beneath her rigid hands,
The bird song against the morning air,
Simple and uncomplicated,
The cool, misty air, a drink of relief
From the drowning compression of these cerebral wings.
And there, deeper than these wondering eyes,
The essence of the wood beneath her fingers,
Or the trilling of morning's song,
Is the whisper...

In the thoughts, in the dreams,
In the night and in the dark,
In the dawn and in the sea,
And yes, ever in the light
From the tears of the stars ...
You are.

Aging

Flaccid skin and memories
Wilting in the high noon sun.
Youth long- flown away on trembling autumn wings.
So impertinent and unkind time has become
Leaving me far behind in winter's unforgiving flare.

Gone and lost the vitality I once ignored,
Forgotten to all but this tired mind.
What began in innocence
Clock has wound back again full circle.

Is yesterday today? Or today lost in yesterday?
The moments blur and fade,
Then surface from the deep waters and flare.
Sudden bursts of clarity! ...
Then all recedes again like tides in the mist.
How fleeting new flames flicker and waver
In life's unrelenting gale.

So my mind seeks to think of finer things,
Finer times and a kinder world
Like the fresh blush of early morning
As the red dawn stains the grass,
How the nightingale sings,
And the soft flap of barn owl's wings...

Amber fields of fireflies,
Laughing and dancing in their flickering light,
Sun-ripened grass drifting fragrant scents across the air,
Hickory-smoke and cherry-wood
From a lazy-embered pipe.

Ornamental dishes lined up like ancient knights,
Fluttering shadows strobe their face
Cast through open windows and billowing lace curtains
Old perfume, antiquated, but loved.
Like rose petals tucked inside a scroll-top desk.

Blue gas flames whooshing to kiss a cast-iron skillet
Still warm from last tea-kettle.
Flour and buttermilk being washed from wizened hands,
Hands that felt like tissue paper and sugar
As my own now, blue-veined and white,
Eyes that once looked on me with love,
Admired my youth and my innocence.
They are now reflected in, now become my own.
As I gaze upon little faces that smile back at me
As I once smiled up at hers.

Tree on a Hill

As the sky drips gray-blue
Off your knobbly branches,
You cry into the clouds
Jagging the fluffy edges,
Dashing the wisps to pieces.

You reach up as your toes dive deep
Remembering decades and hollow years.
The brightness, the shadows the sadness,
The joy of life as winter melted into melody,
Birdsong among your branches.

Edging nearer to the horizon
As light slips below the stars,
Drawn to the fleeting warmth,
Gradually covered in night's blue shadows,
Drooping softly into the turf in darkness...

Cold twigs uncurling slowly as the sun awakes,
Tickles your fingertips with golden hope,
Thaws the night from within toughened skin
Until dawn blazes brightly and greets you
And you shower the shadows down
Across the dappled dew.

Where I Got the Scars

They are road maps to the moments of life
That are best forgotten
But are remarkable, indelible, ugly
Like the ruined topography of a mountainside.
Glaciers of a different time carved out pieces,
Left a puckered trail, a stain
Against the surface of my soul.

Where did my scars come from?
My vision blurs to a swirling vortex of faces,
Pictures, places
Sucking me down like water down a drain.

Gone.
The pillar of my entire world.
First memories of 'tickle monsters' and laughter.
Being tossed into the wide-open sky
And caught by strong hands.
Reduced to an unfamiliar face made of wax
Cold to the touch in a padded box.

Pressed beneath the weight of mother and child,
Rootless, aimless, wandering alone in a sea of grief
Where I dreamed of his face,
Of the way he'd made me feel
Like a princess in a fairy tale world,
And not comprehending that the crystal palace had fallen.
Every dream must shatter.

A child afraid of the dark,
A shadow against the wall.
The phantom hovering over her,
Ragged breathing and pain.
A nightmare she found, as she grew older
Was not a dream.
Hiding behind her older sister,
But she was a child too.

Playing in the fields and along the stream
Fantasy was the escape when the world was too real.
More than a child's imagination,
A child's secret to hide away
Beneath the grasses and wild flowers
Inside the dark drainage tunnel,
Inside the abandoned spring house.
Forgotten, lonely for it, but relieved.

Creating her own nightmares as she grew older,
Anger, defiance, bitterness her defenses.
As a wounded animal she put up her defenses
And ran away, ran away
From the shadows that had haunted her as a child,
As a youth,
Memories she could not escape.

Coldness to mask the vulnerable warmth,
Indifference to mask the longing,
Anger to mask the pain,
Solitude to mask the endless voices,
Dreaming, as ever, to mask reality.

Inviting a new monster in
To frighten away the old.
Left just as empty, just as cold
In a world of confusion, noise, and fear.

Until the day a new silhouette appeared
on this bleak horizon
Who said her ugliness was beautiful,
That the air could be cleaner,
That she was worth more than her scars.
They don't define, they embolden.
They mark her passage as landmarks,
not roadblocks.

And so my vision clears
My wounds begin to heal.
I touch my fingertips to the face inside the mirror

And know I am marked.
But not as a damaged child or a broken stranger.
I am marked as a warrior,
I am marked as strong,
I am marked as a survivor.

As gold must be refined,
So I have passed through the fire
Stronger, more beautiful, more unique.
My fingers trace the white raised lines,
Badges of honor.

This is where my scars came from.

Celtic Dream

Across meadows drunken in silver
Besotted by the dewy eyes of daisies in the moon
And jeweled orbs resting
Like scattered pearls amidst the grass,
The pan-flute sings its lullaby.
And I, too lost to dreaming
To really grasp these gauzy shadows,
Am simply carried by its verse.

Melody flows like water,
Like the currents of an evanescent, seasoned,
Soft, drawing, longing you sing to me.
Wind flows through reeds against the river,
Through the grass, the stars, the trees.
Satyrs dance beneath the harvest moon
While standing stones cast pillar shadows.

Rhythm flow and drum-beat quicken,
Fluttered beats of frenzied heart.
Flute hurry and trickle and dance
Like water splashing in a fountain
Falling over blackened stone
Like quicksilver in the dark.

Persevere

The last few drops of sweetness
Drip off my lips and are gone.
Honey slowly cooling.
Slowing... congealing in the shadows.
Hope lifted me elated to the heavens
Then let me come drifting slowly down.
I reach...I reach for those elusive stars
Whose twinkle I had twirled in my fingers.
I see them wink at me mockingly
From the ground on which I lie.

And yet I fight. I fight to regain the purchase
Which I so tenuously held,
Which I've fought for tooth and nail.
I clench my teeth with the effort,
I hang on as my fingernails break.
I will not give in to the relentless midnight in my mind!

Take away my midnight, and I will remember the sun.
Take away my shackles, and I will fly higher.

The Role of Black

Ever the tragic figure in the shadows,
I don't know how to be anything else.
A figment, a wraith, a ghost to the minds of the pragmatic,
Too ephemeral and wispy to amount to much,
Not in the estimation of those who see only solidarity,
Who cannot sink deeper than their cold, thick skins.
I linger always beneath the surface of their reality.

At death's door, they see me before the tolling of the bells.
They see me and weep because in me they are alone,
In me, their tears turn to ash,
Their lives to cinders,
Their achievements to smoke.
And I will outlast them as the harbinger at their door.
I am patient as I wait.

I am not the most joyful of companions,
I am the first to say it.
But neither am I the most hopeless.
(I will never admit to that.)
I am the shroud and the midnight, and the raven.
But I am also the quiet before the dawn,
And the wrinkle in time's fabric.

Without me, there would be no sun.
Without me, there would be no relief from the day.
Without me, there would be no...
No echo in the cave of your heart.
Echoes bring change as ripples carry secrets.
Sweet whispers find their home in my arms.

I am the silk and shadow and seductive lure of dreams.
I am the velvet that stains the sky like ink,
That lingers 'round the clouds
And threatens from afar,
But warns of the impending storm,
Carries the cadence of the thunder.
Without me, they would not know the beauty of dawn.

Yet they run when they see me coming.

I am the mascara smeared beneath your eyes,
The obsidian shimmer of a deep lake,
Your first companion when you close your eyes
And I allow you to dream while wide awake.
Blue as the egg of the robin,
Fading the sky to black as the sun dissolves away.
I cool the brutal glaring of the white sun of blindness
Resting there in the very center of your eye.

Only the Best I Wish for You

I give you the moon
That glistens on your shoulders,
The platinum sheen in your electric eyes.
I give you the taste of sunshine.
Warm upon your smile. The scent of heat upon skin.
The sweetness of my tears in your hair.

I paint, for you, a thousand pictures
Of trees in the sunset, of blue skies, of hope.
Of the dying hum of song-birds in their nest
As daylight quietly fades to silk and shadow
And I hush your restless wandering
With restful sleep, my hand over your brow
My whispers in your ears for company.

I give you a million wishes
To blow like dandelion seeds against the wind.
I smile, I dance, I exalt in your freedom,
Waltz in the shadow cast by the sun.
I hold its hand and waltz in its mirrored gaze,
Give you the words to say to hush the wind
Until it blows itself out and you are safe in my arms.

And we dream together
Like waves skip along the sea.
We fight together
As lovers ward off an army of doubts
But your face forever cast in silver
Rubs the lining out of the clouds,
Turns away to fight the world alone.

And still, I give you the moon
As dawn turns to silver in the sky
And the jaded lark forgets its song.
Along the banks of possibility, you pull further
Until all that you once hoped has shattered:
Silver shards of who you once were.
Silver shards of who you still could be.

Ink and Feathers

With a black felt-tip pen,
I wrote out the lines that swelled inside
But could never get past my lips
So that others could read what was not understandable
Any other way
A living, breathing scattering of words
On arms, on hands, on pale skin
A caricature of ink and page.

The graceful lines of pen-stroke
The gentle way they curved around my skin
Expressed an elegance painstakingly defined
In a soul almost too complex to decipher
Designed through breath, through heartbeat,
through unspoken whisper
A thought, a feeling that filtered in through too-seeing eyes
Echoed back against the inner walls of my being
And radiated outward again in terrifying sympathy

Ripples. Ripples in a pond.
The flickering images of sight and sound
As they wash over and through me.
A novel written against the blood and bone,
The sinew of me few senses can see
A part of, yet distant,
Quietly drifting on conflicting currents.
Feathers dancing on the breeze.

I lift a hand to touch your face.
Your eyes see into me and mine stare back through you.
We meet somewhere in the middle.
In the mish-mash of two beings blending
In a whirlwind of color and feeling
Leaning forward, your lips brush mine
And softly, softly I dissolve
In white feathers over silver fields.
Falling into darkness my mind creates
To expand its own universe.

Blow away.
Blow away home
Scattered dust of morning light.
Dissolve into winds of increasing frenzy.
And when you have finished your storming,
Wrung every last drop of passion out of the light,
Fade into the shadows that grace the hair
Of a figure unknown and unheard.

Sapphire Shadow

Her ears twitch with the sound
Of laughing glass in the breeze:
Wind chimes clinking like a chandelier,
Water droplets falling into a still pond.

She lifts her nose to the wind
Catches juniper, grass, and wildflowers,
Sun-warmed dandelions and sweating trees.

Tell-tale traces of dust and cedar trees
Keen the senses that make her body quiver.
Profound the deep of her eyes.
She looks at you oddly
as your rocking chair creaks nearby.
She looks at you like a one-winged bird
might look at the sky.

How exquisite, a wisdom is caught up in blue,
In the soulful way she gazes at you
Coal dusted with powder
As though her darkness was buffed by the moonlight.

Angular, soft,
Dark triangles in the sun glow
Quiver and flicker like wire sensors
Perked up in curiosity.

Traipsing on the porch steps
Gaily, graceful stride,
Amateur predator,
Light-footed dancer across these somber skies.

Sad, for no greater reason
Than the fact that the light steadily falls,
So she is scooped up and cradled ...
The softest shadow of them all.

This Wee Girl

I

She had eyes that read the summer
Like a dusty book, old and worn
Saw the beauty in its hot scent
In the baking of earth, and grass, and flower
Over time and weathering seasons
The fading wood of the window frame
The smoothness of the grain inlaid with old dirt

Yet it compressed her to the size of the ant
That hurried just there outside her window
Carrying weight that seemed far too heavy
For the fragile, the tiny and insignificant
Shoulders small and unprepared
For such weight as the years
Those ageless eyes carried

The quiet times were the easiest
Yet they stretched on like the miles of highway
That beckoned her to travel far
Far away from a cage made of suppression
Made of good intentions and feeble tries at nurturing
Like a dry grape on a wilting vine
Whose juice was drained out of season

So far from these heavy bars
The sky beckoned with the readiness of flight
Pathways stretched on like enticing secrets
Roads her mind often traveled
Leaves blown dry and brittle
Senses thirsting for autumn rain
How she longed for wiser hands to gather her in

Breathing the sweet air of youth
Shackled as a butterfly to the ground
Pinned against a black-velvet board

Screaming for her chance in the sky
And despising the fears that kept her there
What was action compared to words?
But still, she kept her silence while her wild eyes roared.

II

The cacophony of silence
The fireworks of souls
That poisoned the brilliant sky she sought
And beat at her like shrill shrieks in the night
The blinding of a grief so final
When her world was made up of moments of time
Glimpses of daylight that some would call childhood

Images glimpsed in a glass
The transparent soul of others eyes
Reflected back in her x-ray heart
So much for so little
When her lips remain silent and her heart cries
Wanting to hold those who should hold her
Wanting to love as she has always needed to be loved

Walking down a solitary pathway
Dust like the faerie dust of her dreams
Billowing up like silver fog to sweep by
Like the misty vale of other worlds
Sound muffled but for the plaintive cry of her silence
She lifts her arms up to invisible hands that hold her still
In the confines of her memories, her dreams of yesterday.

III

Pictures on a faceted stone
Rainbow colors on a farcical screen
She raises her hand to smear the raindrops
That trickle down the window's cheeks
A world that belongs in her mind

A mind that belongs in another world
She smiles for the escape
Strange, newly familiar landscapes

Her fingers trail the ink of a thousand thoughts
Swirl in colors like oil in a puddle
Beauty, peace, adventure, hope
Family, all cradled up warm and alive on this canvas
Rocked into vibrant life by the temerity of her dreams
A passion undimmed by the harsh realities
Of noise, of grief, of life

Awe and wonder and the joy of discovery
Set her soaring to unheard of skies
Eclipsed by the brilliance of distant sunsets
Flight, freedom, and expression
Escape ... from the lonely corner
Where she'd huddled for so long
Companions of clouds and butterflies
And forgotten lullabies
Little Alice lost in her own wonderland

Boastful her innocence
The unflagging spirit
Beyond the contempt of encroaching maturity
Defying practicality for something infinitely practical
Survival
Through fantastical escape
Creating the world where her mind so often dwells.

Robin Red

Teach me to fly on lighter wings
Teach my voice to carry far
Teach my heart to flourish with hope
As spring melts the long chill of winter
And you with the bright jewel of the sky
Born on soft, amber breast
Find the call home welcome and fresh

Black seed pearl eyes, unfathomable
Bright blue as the sky your treasured orbs
That crack and begin
Break and make whole
The circle wound round again

You ushered in death
But with it new life
Papa's favorite sight to see
Before the cancer claimed too much
Took him so far from me
Forever in flight now, he wished for so much
For those he had left behind

And now in my weakness, in my breaking
Time makes me a child again
Who dreams, who hopes, who longs to be as free
And sees the seasons roll over again
This change, this renewal
Through dreams too long shuttered
For you, always for you

Reborn in the spring-time of this year
Time may have forgotten you
But it has not finished yet with me
And reborn I will rise again
And fly with freedom with you

Indifferent Shores

How fleetingly the heart so fickle flies
And rests and breaks on indifferent shores

White Curtain

The shadows behind the snow
Shrunken people pass
Like phantoms behind a gauze curtain
Muted, darkened
Bereft of their terrifying power

Standing as fluffy sentinels
Catching in its corners the drifting snow
Skyscrapers catch their breath
And shiver
Dressed in feather strokes of white

My solitude yawns wide
Like the mouth of this winter storm
The cold blanket matches
The tattered veneer within
Leaves me trembling
As two realities collide

Summit

Terribly deep the draw of your eyes
Blue and silver and green
So far away the gaze from my own
And I am so lost
Without the memory of your touch
I will willingly drown in the beauty of you

Your steppes glisten in the light
Of a higher sun and a cooler breeze
I cannot fight long against the headwind
That whistles from your dangerous smile
But I will tumble in the gale and not fight to be free
Captive to the longing held tight within my dreams

While you soar and survey below
I lift my face to heaven's voice
And hear the thunder round your summit
Reaching, reverberating down to me
So high above me, you stand
So far below you, I kneel

A servant to the break-winds
That ravage my bracing form
Insignificant and small, I submit
To the vast nothing and everything
Captured in your prismatic gaze
The coolness of your caress

Adrift

I see the water a gunmetal blue
As I sail far away
From my memories of you
The light in the sky is a delicate rose
Streaked through with crimson
The color of a soul that bleeds
Into oceans of white-washed skies
That weep broken tears over me

The voice that echoed like thunder
Now rings in my mind like hollow laughter
Taunts our final goodbyes
And I alone, left without you
Left without the hope you lit in my spirit
Like a sun that has been doused by cold midnight
A bright star washed over with a tidal wave of despair
I release my raft to the swallowing tides
Of my own free will

I was once so enthralled just to look at your face
To see a smile that made my heart flutter
Lighten and take wings
The kiss that warmed me to my toes
Like cinnamon Inside the steaming mug
Heat a shield against the winter
And your arms to hold me
And promise that we would never change

A penny for a moment
Glowing like copper in the sun
While with bated breath I blew my wish
Like dandelion seeds into the wind
That you were not just a dream
A figment of an over-active imagination
But then I awoke beside an empty pillow
Cold in the morning chill to be so alone

The smile I never really knew
The touch that lingers though never enough
To penetrate the skin, to warm the darkness away
To soothe the aching emptiness around my heart
You were just a dream away,
A gleaming shadow in the night
Now you fade... you fade away...
Like starlight with the coming dawn
My one-time, lost lover of yesterday

Fly, fly away little starlings
Who'd sung over us while it would last
Fade into backgrounds of soft and white
And leave me to my cloudy sea
And my stormy skies

Embers

Scattering like ashes
The remains of this day
Staring into the embers of what was
Praying that a phoenix fate awaits tomorrow

Storms in the Mirror

Drops fallen from a metamorphic sky
Form into a puddled rainbow

Time swirls these memories
Slow by the moment
Faster by the year
Makes life churn by as quickly
Or as slowly as it pleases

The gray in the sky
Matches the gray of my crown
Earned perhaps by thought or deed,
More likely just by chance
Perhaps only in the feeling
Not in the reality of it

The drudgery of waking
To a world gone mad with grief
To anger, to hate, to bitterness
The clock's hand makes such slow progress
Yet in an instant, years have passed

Endless days held side by side
Noticing the reflections
The same pictures painted different colors
The ferocity growing intense
What we thought was crazy
Looks peaceful in comparison
Yet so much the same
We had dreamed of so much more...

When all we could say
Was dream, dream, dream
To escape the silent screams
That warred in every mind
That exploded every night in the quiet hours

Life takes on a rhythm

A pulse as yet not quite stilled
The rises and fallings
Of a people crying out
For the heartache and injustice of it all
That so many have fallen
Who should have remained
And so many live
Who deserve a worse fate

Where is the answer that violence seeks?
Where is the answer to the desperate questions?
From the way the sky rumbles
I think You are angry too
And You are not silent, only weeping
As the sky sheds Your tears

Fiery Sky

Morning spreads her fire across the sky
Memory burns the innocence

Flute Song in the Forest

A lone flute on a quiet day
Soft, somnolent and slow
Lonely and lovely it sings its song
To a stranger's breeze

At times so low and deep
Steals your breath with its fervent heart
At others high and whimsical
Spreading joy and electric energy
Through veins stiffened by torpidity

How long has it been
Since a distant light sought
To bring life into the misty shadows?
So long I had forgotten the rhythm of breath
The song of summer
The sound of the trees in their rustling
The smell of the sun as it graced the land
The deep, rich earth at its surface

I begin to remember
As the melody plays on
And its breath echoes along hollow corridors
Of my mind, of my spirit

I remember the dawning of day
And the cool of those purple mornings.
I remember the snow melting red along the caps
Of blue mountains lost in mist and shadow
Forgotten by the sun and only earning its passing stain

I remember fairies as they once danced
In linked rings about the wooded floor
Their fingers intertwined like the braided vines
That draped gracefully round them
The flowers that threaded through their hair

I recall, just faintly in this half-awake state

The soft coo of dove voice
As they droned a lullaby to the twilight
And said 'Farewell' and 'Good Morning' each day

I've forgotten why I fell asleep...
How determined I was to dream away the despair
The emptiness of being alone
I remember then how loneliness can take hold
Can take root and bind you to the ground

The soothing whir and whistle
The low swoops and lyrical flight
Of the flute's tune
Draws me out of my languid, lazy dream

There is life, there is beauty still
To find amidst the shadows
Like dew on dry meadows
And it calls me, it sings to me
From the lilting throat of this fluted verse

It awakens the softer heart of the beast
Who had wallowed too long in the torment
Of sadness and morbidity
Of endless, guilt-ridden silence

It raises me up from what was darkness
To what now has become green and fragrant
And alive
The curtain of her hair parts the curtain
Of the surreal smile I wear and my own delight

Once a love song, once a lament
Once a voice crying for peace
Unchained by this melody, I come awake
And I rise to live again

Seaside

The breeze sifts the sand through layered skies
Sand softly ticks and nuzzles my skin
Cocoa butter and brine and summer
Waft across to me like a lullaby

The pound and the hiss
The waves curling over
Falling with colossal thunder
Thrust forward, then drawing back

The sun would taste like melted butter
Lemon in the morning
Browns me to a nice toasty brown
Sugar and cream well baked

Endless soft-beat of wings
Lonely cries in the sky
Circling over-head
Trying deftly to catch my eye

Cool blue and winter-green
Makes my over-heated mind steam
Cleansing waters filter away real life
Churn the tides of ancient days my way

Foam collects little bubbles
Air pockets to reflect the sun
Smoothing the sand
Like fine snow to glass

Drifting away on effervescent dreams
Near and away
Fickle and shy they say
The tide undulating behind my shoulder

Memory Fades

It was their daddy's painting
His favorite mountain, his first love
Lovingly wrought in oil and charcoal
Shadowed, smeared, and shaped by his fingertips

He'd sit and sketch
And smell of cedar shavings
Pipe puffing fragrant smoke
His fingers were stained black

'Even the shadows have life.' he'd say
Left for the imagination to wander
'Tell me its story. Sing me its song.'
It broadened the scope of my mind

Long years have passed since he was here
He's passed on to nevermore
But left his fingerprints behind
In coal and oil

Relegated to an abandoned attic
Draped in white sheets
Like the cobwebs of time
Folded over quiet wisdom
Lost to our memories
Lost to time
Moldering in the silence
Alone

I'd seen the pine-trees on the green hills
In summertime in the mountains
I knew each spike and frond
Of their landscape and tree-line

I knew how the sun rose through mist
Thick as smoke
And turned the sky red and orange
And how that color fell among the trees

I saw the forest kindle and burn
By some unknown, careless hand
I saw the black smoke rise up
Like greedy, grasping hands

And when we came and the attic was cleared
We pulled out this last reliquary of memory
Their daddy's painting in oil and coal
Smeared and forgotten

'Great grand-daddy used to paint.'
'He used to smoke a pipe and smell of cedar.'
'His fingers were always stained black.'
Time rubbed out the thoughts, the memories
Fire rubbed out his trees.

Farewell to Autumn Skies

The morning sun weeps tears of dew
Upon my waking bereft of you.
The sinking moon falls with a sigh
It waited long, but now must die.

And I upon my pillow damp
Close fast my eyes against the stamp
Of loneliness, harsh and bitter
Of waking to find all I had feared was true

It was a dream, a waking dream
The moments and hours caught in auburn hair
Like leaves battling wind in the fall
I beat my fists against brick walls

Of bitterness and smoky embers
Of fall and chilly stares
Tasting the dry crumble of leaves
That smolder in passions shadow

To me you are the maiden ghost
Who haunts my sleep and my waking alike
You dance away in streams of smoke
Yet close as fog wrapping around me in embrace

I see your smile in the barren trees
That were once so full of color and life
Now ripped to bare skeletons
In this cold, pretentious breeze

To fly you dreamed on silver winds
With feathers much too frail
I weep tears of mercury at your fall

To an empty world you've left me
The joy here a stranger to me
A hope I cannot take part in
A bland face of fantasy

But for you, I swallow the sky
In one great, consuming gulp
For you made me see its beauty
And I carry its empty depth in my gut

Through these tears
I ask no pity
I seek no great reprieve
Loss is now my company
My last farewell to you

Warmth in the Grey

Walls stained by sunset
Beneath a shadowed sky
Water bleeding red
Beneath the sun's blood-shot eye

Grey and colorless
The ground beneath the keep
The warmth within the stones
Surviving though it weeps

Like a dream half-remembered
One too good to forget
That paints its way across my mind
As the ragged sun in my mind sets

A warm hearth that refuses to relinquish its cheer
In a cold and weary land
Incapable of leaving
You hold on with cold, numbed hands.

Thorns Against the Sunset

Thorns against the sunset
Bleeding ink on russet rose
Jagged as the needles on its stem

Violence on a pretty page
A jolting shadow in the light
A stain of trauma jading innocence

Or Conversely...

The fog of delusion
Against this brilliant night sky
Incredulity and madness
interrupting my dreams

Bursting and disorienting flash
Taunting laughter bubbling within
My cool, gentle sky of stars

Sea Witch

I was the voice behind her Muse
I called forth the wind behind the sails
And harnessed the power behind the sea

I turned melody into discordant cries
And reduced the needy into a shuddering garden
I set the insolent in their place

I enraptured the prince with borrowed siren song
And bid the king pay a borrowed price
Only to steal his payment

I reached out with grasping arms
Tentacles that ensnared and captured
To strangle beauty, to possess power, to mock hope

I gave voice to the four winds
And caused it to blow
'Round distant hills as a bereft banshee

I became as a goddess
Towering above the waves
And laughed at heroism in spite

I took up the visage of an innocent maid
To seduce a fickle prince
What they don't know is ...
That I never let him go

My shadow haunts him still...

Vast Blue Skies

Blue skies
That dome and ripple
That swell overhead
And all around.
A terrific bevy of shaped, puffy clouds
Wink as the sun glints behind

With my arms spread wide
I fall into this endless sea
Flying or falling
In mercy's arms
Jumped out of my own mind
Made the leap with grace

I fall into the open mouth of the sky
And am swallowed whole

Snow Crystals

Icy lace against my window
Chilly drafts along the floor
Powdered sugar as light
As shifting sands

Covering over and renewing
The cold, hard ground
Frosting the icy shell
Preserve and purify

Holding the world in stasis
Until the bitter chaos
Of busyness and work
Soil the covering to brown slush

Churning up the crystalled ground
To mix as slush and gravel
Filth to mar the white
Tracks to print the pristine

Until next I dance in your soft falling
Till next you are sweet on my tongue
Till next you cleanse the world of foggy time
I will dream ... I will dream

Face to the Sun

I throw back my hair
To take in the sun
To let the night be drawn out of me.

The golden glow flows
Through veins made of green
That nourish and beat from a budding heart

I allow the beams to caress my face
Roots that go deep drink of this warm well
From eyes to deep, chilly toes

Fettered to the ground only to naked eyes
My spirit dances balletic and free
Eyes turned heavenward to welcome

The touch of wind brushing the leaf from my cheek
Softening the bark that makes up my shell
Pliant and strong my beautiful brown skin

Spider Queen

Little pearls of starlight
Nestle against your silver strings
The weave of a dreamer
With infinitely practical means

Up to you the tactic to hover or fly
Attached by silken fiber
Billowing in the stream
Of a breeze errant and soft

Dancer of death
Or bearer of news
What exactly does the night say to you
As you work fervently in its silence?

You spin till the sun catches its first beams
Against your laborious knitting
Lighting it with crystalline dew

Then wait for the finding
The unsuspecting meal coming to you

The Muse

Upon these misty, hidden shores
In my mind, in my mind
The beautiful holds its secrets
Under lock, and key and ancient chamber door
Ribbons of water lace the stone castle
Trickle down in silver trails
While out of mountain's green cloak
Stones rise and form in towers and turrets
Secluded in the hollow of the mountains arms

There dwells my lady her arms jewel studded
By many passing moments treasured more fair
Than any king's ransom could purchase
There dwells my hope wrapped up in her silken tresses
Treading footsteps with finer weave
Than a spider weaves her web
Images hewn as gossamer threads
That thoroughly bewitch the mind
Pray tell, pray tell, Lady Waiting
What the muse whispers to you
in this lovely Keep of time?

Ordinary Clouds

From the time my feet first toddled
And my little self began to observe and think,
I noticed the inconsequentially significant
The beauty of normalcy
And wore blinders to the practical practices
Of mice and men.
Like the cart-horse on the corner in reverse
I admired things on the fringes
That practical people would ignore
And did not look straight ahead to where I was going
Or where the straight-ahead path would lead.
Wandering on the little pathways
Walked by those that veered outside the lines
Of expected and inclusive.

A pigeon pecking seeds from the tramp's hand
Who sat alone on a park bench
Became my world of questions
The story that would weave throughout my mind
With question, with sadness, with the loneliness
Reflected back from the cast-off's eyes.
'Are you as weary as your eyes suggest?''
I would question.
'Did you put yourself here as people say
By mistakes, or laziness, or addiction?
Or did life just overwhelm and chastise and blame?
Of what consequence are you and that little park bench
And the pigeon eating from your hand
To any other who passes you by?'
To me, you were more real than the crowds
As I tripped over myself and the curb in my path.

A stray dog who sat alongside the road
Wagging its tail at any who would pass
And be thoroughly ignored,
Fascinating and heartbreaking to me
As a death along the fringes of my child's mind.

I would think to feed and to pet and to love
The innocent eyes looking back up at me
As though in feeding a stray,
I fed the aching in my own soul
As my mother tugged my hand
And pulled me away from the mutt
On the side of the street
'Pay attention to where you're going!'

A performer on the stage held me enraptured
Long after the curtains had shut.
To others a brief holiday, there a moment and then gone
To me a lingering dream, a magical world
Where I longed to belong and be a part of
'It's not real, it's pretend!' they told me with disgust.
To me, it had been more real and much more desirable
Than pulling my head down out of the clouds.
Even the clouds themselves there were fascinating
Where dreams could take form and feelings take shape
And be soft, and white, and out of reach
to anyone other than me.
Nothing could damage dreams so soft and so high
So set apart from the pairs of feet
way down on the ground
Where they told me to plant mine alongside.
The performer must see those clouds as I do
And have the courage to grasp them
In spite of other's scorn.
How happy they looked to be living
with their eyes on the clouds!

How captured I was
By the street-barker who called out his wares with a grin
But whose eyes continually cried
Like a dusty clown surrounded by gags and goofs
Who could only mourn his lost dog on an empty leash.
Was it the stray I had seen the day before
Who'd been ignored?
Was their being apart what caused such sadness?

'It's just a show. It's just pretend.'
But it could be true, it could connect.
They were both the same,
Weren't they?

A tiny padlock and tinier key
Promised great secrets and great enticement.
It could open up a world that only I could enter
Where wishes were not only accepted
They were encouraged
And my face was viewed kindly, not in accusation.
The key to a universe where everyone wore smiles
And everyone said 'Hello' instead of passing by,
Where friends were united and no one ignored
And clouds were the ordinary order of the day
Not only for dreamers like me.

Mama

Laying down against the soft, cool earth
Grass still lightly warmed by the sun
Fills me with the sweet smell
Of dirt and grass and life

My eyes travel up to the sky above
Stare into infinity's blue-ringed eye
Work cloud shapes into dreamy form
Soft, and discerning and white

Coming home to you
Is remembering these leisurely days
Taking a dandelion in small hand
And letting the breeze scatter its softness into pieces
That is what time has done to that innocence...

But still your arms are open and near
No matter how far I am from the child we once knew
Still you will press my head against your breast
When tears have no comfort but your love

It was you who first dried those tears
Who saw potential behind every mistake
Who believed in me when I didn't believe in myself
And over the years that has never changed

Days pass too quickly
Years fall like tissue-thin leaves on autumn trees
Whose branches can scarcely keep hold of their trunk
Life scatters us haphazardly like fall's smoky breath

Fragile and thin your hands have become
Thin blue veins threading through the pale
As those crepe-like leaves once lush and green
In summer's past, then autumn's requiem have failed

Eyes full of wisdom with lines alongside
As though the years passing wires

Have carved their web-work here most thick
They still stare at me with keen understanding
You were and you are my fairy-tale queen
Become only more surreal and more lovely with time
Which may have faded your body,
But not your eyes
Not your embracing spirit

I acknowledge what strength you had to possess
To carry on, make your mistakes, and watch mine
Yet still carry ever on and draw out the lessons
To teach me and leave your own cares behind

These things you give me
Could I ever understand?
Ever fully impart to my child?
Never as fully or as perfectly as you

You tell me your love was imperfect
You made your own mistakes
But little mistakes seem so small to me now
I allow you to feel your regrets
Because you allow me mine

The smell of old books and worn out bindings
Tea on cool nights and lemons on the warm
Fresh soap in the bathroom dish
And iodine on scraped knee
Soup stock simmering on the stove

Cookies in the oven
Pledge in the air
Fresh folded laundry
On your only rocking chair

I'd sit by your side as we shelled peas
And you'd tell me stories of grander days
Then sing me to sleep by the fireside
The rhythmic rocking of the chair

And your heart my lullaby

In my blind eyes...
In my blind, wishful eyes...

Ever you were longed for
Ever you were there
What I needed and never had

'What dreams may come...'
I heard a masterful muse stipulate
And the dreams did come
Ever so sweet and often

I lived in a land of never no more
Where the wishes most dear are kept
Under strict lock and key
Whatever guardians be
Grown more elusive and strong with age

A mirror, a name
Sometimes close to the same
On whom could you blame
My lonely heart?

Always when I close my eyes
There you'll be
Always as far or as near as need be
And I'll hear your lullabies ever and on
As I close my eyes to sleep

Rain Down

Pin-pricks dimpling the flat calm of the pond
Ants crowding in hurried armies along the grass-line
Air heavy with a bitter, coppery tang
The trees lift skyward fingers for coming relief
The ground cracks her dry maw to welcome raindrops in
To ease the passing of life through her rusty veins

Rain
Let it rain down

Purple is the sky that is bruised and battered
Yet heals through this purging storm
Lightning slice apart the sky
So ribbons of starlight can glisten in the tears
The drops that gather in the hair of trees
And whisper softly through the breeze
Jewel the spider web and awaken the besotted mind

Rain
Let it rain down

Elegant Storm of Sky and Sun-ripe

The sun flashes on chrome
Wheels that turn and chug and labor
Up along the glistening oil-blackened engines
Breathing in the great labor of momentum
For your sacrosanct tonnage
Steam issues forth from steel nostrils
Announces an odd 'hello'

Booted foot brushed by lace skirts descends trestle stairs
And lady elegance holds out a hand
To be supported downward
Bedecked with ribbon and flower and feather
Delicate and lovely as a floating swan she moves
She turns her graceful head and flashes electric eyes

Silver lightning strikes its barbed head between
Eyes of crystal and eyes of dark sienna
Molten chrome heat beneath a red sky
Earth and summer sky meet beneath the haze
Yellow dust clouding up in dreamy billows
Redolent of sulfur wisps curling up from hot waters
Dissipating only enough for the magnetic storm to flicker

Controlled she comports herself
As a glass statue tip-toeing through projecting rocks
He flowing as smoothly as the wild river careening by
And the soft sand that gathers on its banks
Bejeweled with silt-like diamond passing as softly
As the flutter of green leaves showing veined silver bellies
Different as morning and midnight meeting in the skies
Passionate as sheet lightning over the prairie grass

Letters penned by oak and tree
As milkweeds fall from green-shadowed sky
Pen-tip pressing to clean parchment
As a fingertip touching the smooth line of jaw
And flower petal lips

She dreams of love by candle-light
And perfume scented water
He seeing his phoenix rise up into the moon
And ride ghostly white wings through the dark
She shivers and leans back from the window shutter

Gloved fingers untying leather cord
Binding parchment pages
Unfolding a letter as a sky unfolding its stars
Breath catching in her throat in a staggering pulse
Purity, delight, and innocence
Tingling over the nerves along her arms
Rippling brush of unknown desire
Against her too-pragmatic mind
He kisses the breeze
As a fluttering bird transmits his longing
How the sunlight makes her hair sparkle
Like russet honey in the sun

At night as the moon filters her dreamy, jaded beams
Gazelle meets running stag in fur-lined shadows
Beneath her gaze
Earth and sky embrace in completion
Of a prophecy told long ago
Sun and sand and water converge
To fulfill the baffled thoughts
And letters penned beneath the same moon
Lay a blanket for their bed
Owls sing a lover's refrain and passion bears her teeth
As misery makes its way past longing to surrendered joy

Held beneath the stars the swan ceases her flight
And the stag slows his hurried wandering
Trails his fingers over the elegant curves
Of letters and words
Responses gathered in like water,
Soft as moss to his thirsty ears
Shuddering in the shadows she is still against her fears
How the long days fade... how they fade...

Till the sunlight rises and cloaks the dream
In reality burning bright

Dear guardian of my heart,
My journal penned by morning light
Tread not on paths laid out by well-made plans
Forge bravely on to places unseen
Places forged by your own hands.

Useless Things

Mama cried in the other room
While mourning strangers offered her comfort.
The radio played softly in the hall.
I was just a child, not understanding
The earth-shaking change, but knowing
Knowing the world was a little off-kilter
A little less bright today

No one heard the radio play,
But I wanted to dance in its melody
To dance and distance myself
From this unasked for interruption
Of life, of normalcy.
And I longed for daddy's lap,
The smell of his cigars, the soft whiskers of his face

They said I could not see him again...
They said war was a bad thing...

Unable to bear the monstrous weight
Of adult misery and grief,
I retreated to my room and went to find my own comfort.
I found it in daddy's cigar box.
The one he'd made just for me
Filled with useless little things he knew I'd treasure
Things he'd collected for me

My own monument to him would be
What he'd already given to me.
I filled the cigar box with brightly colored stones
I got my pocket-knife out
and chiseled a crude monument stone
From the plain block of wood
And set it pride of place in the stones

With matches and crayons, I marked out a pathway
To the little flag that I leaned against the memorial stone

Standing back to view the effect
I felt a strange compulsion.
Not knowing why I did it,
Except it's what daddy always did when he saw the flag
I stood up straight, put my hand to my brow
And I saluted for freedom.
I saluted for daddy.
I saluted because I could.
Because daddy had left me a box full of useless things
That were not so useless at all.
He'd left me treasures that I would one day understand
Had everything to do with a little, American flag

Sonnet

Like a dancer waiting to be dressed in morning dew
The dragonfly dips her feet in ink
And flutters across the page.
She brings color to emptiness
Life to bare page

The house sparrow singing outside my window
Adds joy to the winds that whisper
Softly in my ear
Trills and directs the rhythm and the song
Till melody and harmony collide in perfect resonance

The rising sun stains the lower ceiling
Of a morning cloud bank
It stains my mind with indelible ink
Sings beauty over my mind
Rock and tree and creature become a living chorus

And I, so small and quiet, just an observer really
Of this grand tapestry
Sit and reflect and revel in the silent cacophony
Of a million living voices
So often ignored, only heard when one really listens

However small, each one calls to me
Minute in their individual existence
But vibrant, passionate and breathing
Strong in eloquence as well as heart
Patient scribe breathless and closed-eye

Drawing from an inkwell with a name
Nobody else can read
Story and life flow like the blood of heroes surrendered
A tale not often told and just as often forgotten
Reflections in the waking dark
Deep blue skies against the moon

A wish, a hope, a dream born on downy wings
Held in trembling hands and spun with ordinary pen
No need to embellish what life has so expertly wrought

I am nothing but the scribe to her genius
The listener to her sonnet
Weeping in the light of her vibrant sun

Sepia Tuned

I let my fingers dance over yellowed keys.
Though I know it is imperfect tone
Still it moves me.
Faded light beams in through long-broken glass
Turns the dust into fairy-dust, gold sparkles in a dream
Sepia toned and faded the world stares back at me.

Memories, memories like the faded photographs
Stacked in a forgotten crate.
Yellowed and ghostly they dull the mind
Into a lovely, archaic dream.

The tired piano follows my lazy fingers
Paints a far-off melody in the air
Round again, back again softly it grows
Echoes from another time.

Here and not here, should I wake or sleep
This flattened image of pale sky
Of sun and sand and horse and rider
Of duels and sienna skies

Tonics and tunics in blue-bottled jars
Intricate stitching on the last
Herbs and haversacks in dry-goods stores
Candies lined up on the shelf.
Pistols and gun smoke and old music reels
The tired music box in my mind.

Tack and post
Light and decay
Smoke rising from a cigar
Whiskey would cure any illness
Or dull the mind to its pain.

Indians with brightly-colored feathers
And savage faces
Contained the deepest hearts

Unfathomable to settlers white minds.
Savagery of will sparked depth of passion
No weaker, no more frightening than they

Into an unbroken wilderness
The faded wagon-tracks led
To fade, to fade ...
The ghostly inhabitants
Of this forgotten day

I play and I play
The melody singing its own melancholy
Through the pianos struck chords so weary

Dust rises up like a mist in the night
Sweeps the memories away.

Approaching Storm

I open the window, un-shutter my heart
And let it rain.
Warmth spills down my cheeks like trailing sunshine
Catches a light within me so bright
It shatters to the touch.

The last pale reflections of day
Catch in the raindrops on the glass
Turns water to crystal, crystal to rainbows.
The rainbows reflect the colors of my heart when I was young.
I will never forget.

Dry wood cracked but smooth beneath my hands.
This windowsill has seen too much weather.
Sun, wind, rain and hail have worn it pale
Calloused and cracked like the skin of my heart.
You can smell the summer in its pores.

Foreboding in the thunder,
Fear in the lightning
Low rumbles of you approach
And steal my breath away.
And you echo so deep it causes a tremor in my chest
As though a bird nested there and was suddenly startled.

Like a ripple in my skin I feel the tension
The onset of this storm
Eyes up, hair lifting
Charging the air like waves of static.
I feel it sizzle and pop in my fingertips.

The wind blows into my lungs and steals my breath away
And I lift my arms to ride its upward swell.
I would fly away and rise on your currents.
Take me higher than this place,
Higher than thought and this aching feeling.
Broken is the mind who has seen too much
Known too much of life.

Like a bird on a wire I long to look down
On this mad world with indifference.
Numbness would weight me to my center
And still the trembling of my soul.
While the shower sprinkled down light like mercury
Dampness like a blanket.

So small, so fragile
Coiffed into a little ball
As a seedling reaching for the sun.
Stretching up and risking the light
For just a little drop of rain.

The silence shatters like broken plate sugar
As I close the window to leave the world alone.
Copper still stings my tongue from the electrified sky.
Light flickers like a weary strobe through the dark.
Darkness rolls in like a wave of the sea
Cold and thundering and deep.

I lay down to watch the movie outside the window
Tired of fighting the storm.
The storm behind my eyes plays like a movie-reel
I no longer care if I am swallowed by the raging beast
As I turn my back to the open door.

Birds In the Courtyard

Harmless harbingers of the dawn
Smoky night brushed away by the strides
Of ghostly wings

Congregating in the golden light of dawn
Watching, waiting, staring with bated breath
The tension thick before that first voice
First laugh filters up from the streets

You assemble in a flock to cackle
To sing or to weep
Like chattering children you move and scurry
Once that fragile shell of morning breaks new

Until the footsteps draw near to reclaim
This courtyard of stone belongs to you
To wing and wind and sun and sky
And eventually ride the sunbeams back
To sleep in lonely hollows beneath the moon

But this glory, this newness
This cool morning mist In that hushed hour
Before the world awakens
This belongs to the whisper of your wings
The fragile fluttering and jostling
Of silence in the crowd

Change

As the colors trickle down my face
Against this pane of rain-flecked glass
I see the years, the days, the hours
Moments that swell and grow like rain
Drops that fall against my soul
Darkening spots against the dry ground
The grey pearl sky to wet my mind

Time left these images behind,
Memories like discarded dreams
Scattered drafts, leaves in a breeze
But I, so afraid to let go,
Cling tightly as a pod to its seeds
As the water trickles its wandering trails
Jagged pathways across my soul

Where was I then? Where am I now?
Questions asked and answered
Or left unfinished, sentences without periods
As time marches its inexorable rhythm forward
A boy grows into a man, a girl to a women
Relentless as each footstep makes gradual progress

Were I still the fragile little caterpillar,
Small and frightened of its own shadow
I could not see myself for what I was, what I am
Nor hope for what I hope will be
Once reborn from this close, confining chrysalis of 'now'
Immediacy and the temporal becoming permanent
Thatched together by the strings of passing days
Becoming the past...

Legs then clung to fragile stems curved as bow-strings
Twisted as wire, but green, alive, and fragrant
Tired of clinging, dropping to a tear as childhood departed
My hopes and wistful longings erected around me a shell
Hurts locked away within my home

Within the dark, secret places I waited... I wait...
Time that hangs so heavy on the pearls of water
On my window cracks thin lines into my outer walls
It widens its gaps merciless and harsh
Numbed I melt and re-form in private night
Knowing the change is coming, fearing it
Yet reaching desperately as the dry well thirsts for this rain

I begin to feel more full as change presses inward
Thrusts outward against the resistance of my fear
Timidity lashed by necessity, by undying hope
To the rhythmic throbbing of my heart
To flourish, to fly I cry in bittersweet sorrow
To feel the winds caress again

Breaking forth as the sun breaks over the mountains
Spilling and stretching tender wings
At once as strong and incorporeal as the dawn
Colors to rival the morning aurora
Condensed, deep and shimmering in newness
Inked across a canvas of such delicate weave

Fluttering open and anew I rise to make my random path
On unsteady legs, unsteady beats of these wings
Wandering but joyful I flicker in the sun-banished shadows
Cast aside the tears of yesterday
Remembering only inasmuch as they comprise the core
Of who I was, what I am, and what I hope to be

Time you march on
Life you change me
Love you transform me
Hope you teach me how to fly
Fragile wings become stronger with every new motion
Every flicker of every new smile

Behind the Eyes

Behind these eyes the world turns slowly
Ever moving, yet standing still
And I move past melting into the colors of the wall
Like a chameleon in the sunset
Who feels the fire, yet casts no blame
Blinded by the passion and the subtlety
You feel the agony and the ecstasy
Dance in the spring rain
Bask in the summer sun
And rest through the long winter

Behind these eyes, there are closed doors
More than one might imagine
Rooms full of scars, veins in the lining that run deep
Like ore; less precious, but no less protected
I can drown in my own mind
In the sea of fervid wandering
Or fade into the shadows of my own silence

I can be a rock-star without a song
Or a gesture-less mime
Content to let the world go by

I can see but not understand
Seek but never find.

White Rabbit

New fallen snow had never been softer
Than the tufted white fur of her coat
An inquisitive nose to wiggle to indicate her placid nature
Or to race in quiet excitement
Her world draped in cool shadows or warm sunlight
Flowers and greens the simplest of fare,
To her the jewels of the earth
Lying down amidst the soft pines and leaves
Their dry, woody aroma her bed
Cuddled against her family, always close, always warm

Light catches her eye and illuminates it like a sapphire
Separates each strand of gossamer white
Sweet puff of a tail to rival the dandelion's silk
Nibble, nibble with cheeks all a tremble
Little can provoke her to worry
Ears laid back in rest, then standing upright as a soldier
To catch the faintest sound on the breeze
Curious or afraid, always interested, intent
Quick as a thought bounding through the grass.

Love's Beautiful Wilting

When you truly love
How can you truly let go?
The love that made you complete,
Has left you wholly broken
The healer and the punisher
The passion and the pain
Grows to a late blooming flower
A wilted rose
Sweetness to cover the stench
Beauty to cover the slow poison of decay

Yet were the heart left unbroken
It would never see the light of day
Nor see the change of renewal and re-birth
Had the flower not wilted
It could never have seen the spring come again
The victory is in the defeat
Dying to self to live again
Breaking to be remade

Life and love, the most fragile of things
Cannot be supported by the paper wings of human trust
It can flicker as the last light of a dying summer
Flutter feebly as the butterfly's dying breath
But it cannot sustain

The translucent veins of the heart run through every petal
Every fiber of our being
The breath of existence pounds like a hurricane,
Cries like the wind
Our being in and a part of
Isolated yet consumed
By the energies and desires that govern our lives

Our dying agony
Our living regret
Our savior and crucifier
Our never-ending lament

Our beautiful melancholy
Our whispered refrain
Our forgotten dreams
And our aching emptiness

Hello, goodbye
Midnight meets morning
Our tortuous healing
And refreshing rain
Never again, once more

Love is a crystal sunrise
That reflects its sparkles onto a dying world
It revives and awakens
Yet hides its thorns beneath its glossy finish
When justice proves false

He has no name, no identity
Aside from the tramp in the street
Unnoticed, unloved, forgotten.
His eyes hold the deepness of forever
Of sorrow and endlessly recurring nightmares
Locked away tightly in some hidden schism of his mind
Wanting to go back, to make amends for the unmendable
But wanting to stay here, far away from yesterday
Even if it is here, on this cold, lonely street
Rather this than that unending nightmare.

To many, perhaps his gaze seems empty
Devoid of meaning or purpose
The same who sneer and shrink from his stench
And see no more deeply than they are seen
Scorned by the very statutes
That would define their own souls

What shadows lie in the meaning of this man
That could not reflect on us?
What demons lie in wait in our privileged shadows
That he has not known before?

Perhaps it is he who has a more worldly perception
Of reality and love and life
Who knows the cruel blows that love encounters
Its loss and its suddenness.

What are your dreams for justice?
Justice once defined his life,
He fought for us and for our future
Now justice has turned cold and turned its back
To watch him fall into despair
To rob him of his future
Where we pass by him finding a justification
Feeling his punishment just.

Patchwork Woman

Faded patches
Tattered stitches
Dust in her hair
As the dust of memories past
Her life in rewind
Yellowed parchments, faded lettering
Leading from empty childhood
To this empty street
Cold, impersonal stone
High towers of imposing wealth
Mockery and indifference
Even disgust
For the likes of her

Eyes are dulled
Of that vibrant spark
That had once marked her of this life
Now she is the dregs of life
Cast off and tossed into the gutter
What she had once been
What she has become
Everything she once knew
Swallowed up by life
Life of a cruel and harsh nature
Left her behind
Alone
Cold
Empty

Invisible yet reviled
Unnoticed yet kicked aside
Was she once you?
Is she what I may be?
Gloves as dirty as the city garbage bin
She rifles through
To her our garbage is a treasure
Reduced to pursuing the most basic necessities of life
A simplicity in her pursuits, her motives

Yet the simple pursuits more complicated
Than my spoiled mind will ever know

Does she have a story?
Did her book have a beginning and an end?
If asked, she would simply stare
Whatever it was then
However it began
It has led here
And here, she believes, it will end.
Dried up as a carrion carcass
The refuge of life
And our darkest, most depressing moments
For her there is no hope
Hope was once an illusion
That has slowly faded
As she has slowly faded
Into the dust of the street...

Merry-Go-Round

Merry go round
Broken down
Round in a circle
Sad calliope sound

Merry go, merry go
Merry go round
How you stutter
Your unearthly sound

Too-sweet smile
Too-pretty face
Cover the stains
With perfume and lace

Dance in the shadows
Play in the light
Fear the day
And love the night

Sugar and spice
Laughter not tears
Shadows fall across
Too many years

Nightmares and dreams
Play in my head
Am I alive?
Or am I dead?

Merry go, merry go
Merry go round
Gnash at the eyes
And fear the sound

Bunnies and bees
And kitty-cats too
Stare at my eyes
Staring at you

Sing to me, smile
Comfort and lie
Truth in my head
Lies in your sigh

Child or minx
Vixen or doll
Love me or leave me
It's your call

Some things were sure
I once believed
Truth was persuasive
Though ill-conceived

Trusting once pure
I forget your name
Could you and I
Be the same?

Don't know what I remember
What I want to forget
All spins around
In my head's net

Merry go, merry go
Merry go round
Dizzy and ill
Pounded into the ground

Child of the Forest

Shining dimly like the light
From some perverse moon
Beauty in illumination
But it is illuminated darkness
A shadow falling on a heart of stone
Whose only dream is to live in the light
While dreaming in black

Tainted innocence
Is innocence still?
Portraying clearly what it once was
And showing just as clearly how it left
And what is now left behind
Silhouette or reflection
Deeper beneath the surface of who you are
Yet a ghostly imprint, fingerprint
Of a life you remember only in dreams
A waking, yet slumbering nightmare

Child of the lonely dark
Foregoing hope of redemption
To cling more tightly still to the memories
Dancing like phantom fireflies
In the flickering film surrounding
Like sunlight dancing on water
A summer day you once knew
Tasting it as clearly as looking through glass
Sweet as sugar
Yet a glimmer, a faint breath
A gasp in the dark
There and back again
Tangible and real and clasped tightly
Then gone...

Memory is but a slow, sticky conglomeration
A loose vapor, clinging cloud
It refuses to ever fall solidly enough to remain
To be found forever

But will not leave you entirely
Lost in its own web
Like a spider spinning its own shroud
Destined for its own demise
Embracing its ill-fated destiny

Scarecrow

Walking along a deserted path
Weed overgrown grass on either side
Cold water pressing in from the river nearby
Laying a hand to my chest
As though to contain the struggling beat
Limbs as numbed as the sticks and straw
The black, lifeless eyes of the scarecrow

Crows make their feet dance
Taunt with their laughter
Just beyond your fixed vision
Could you but uproot the stakes that hold your feet
Raise a raggedy arm that would blow in the wind
Still as a comical statue
Puppet of comic facade
Stitched up by twine and string
Patched and frayed as so many broken places fray
You bleed out through gashes
That no one has bothered to heal

You are the silent sentinel
That watches over the golden waves
Of this summer sea
Who watches the sunlit sky turn from blue,
To gold, to olive green
Then turn purple and sink behind the hills
You are the sky-gazer who reflects the stars in your eyes
And dreams of places beyond
While ever rooted and standing still
Feet on the ground
Head in the clouds

A word to utter would be a tease to the breeze
Undulating the golden wheat
And brushing your legs like feathers
A tear to cry would be to taste the rain
That drops and bends the fair heads
Makes them cower and hide their faces,

Streaming in the summer storm
A song to sing would be the whistle
Of wind gurgling the pond
And whispering through the nearby branches

You are the hollow man
Stuffed with innards far too flammable
To the fire of emotion
The storm of passion or the chill of fear
But you bleed ... you bleed
And you fall in pieces that are tossed apart by the wind
Gradually ripped apart and scattered to an unknown sky
An unknown day

What is it to you the prick of a needle?
The tear of your clothes
Stitches scarring your face, your hands, your feet
Will they contain you forever?
Or will they eventually burst as ripe as new corn
And spill you out like an offering of gold coins
Onto the dusty ground

Bird On A Wire

Bird on a wire
Staring at the rain
Doesn't wanna hear the thunder
Doesn't wanna see the pain
Just rinsing off his feathers.

But it's not easy
To soften lightning's flicker
Its forked tongue, it tears
A jagged rift into the sky
The wind blows colder
Gives a voice to softened rage
Howls about its self-destruction
But isn't it just fine?
It's supposed to be this way
Storm light flashes
Turns the sweet milling faces
Into monsters in the dark
Helpless in despair

Don't think it's easy
To watch them from afar
But when you get closer
Fly to give some aid
Some comfort to their screaming
The storm only strengthens
So you hide yourself away
Close your eyes against the noises
Of a world that's going under
You get accustomed to their pain
You feel it in your blood
As you beat your feeble wings
You smell it as you breathe
And you taste it in the rain
Why can't you look into one's eyes
Without being tainted?
Affected by the strain?
But they pull themselves away

Morning christens
The start of a new day
But you're still mired in their pain
And you can't run away
From what's embedded in your memory
Just can't ran away

So you fold your wings around you
Cover up the gaze
That betrayed you to the curse
Their never-ending bane
And fall from the sky
Like a star that lost its way
Addicted to the love
That turned you to a drunkard
Heady on dismay

Going under
The dark gutter water in the streetlight
Never be a source of cracked reflections
Bouncing back the blackness
Of a broken soul
Never be a thorn inside a glass rose
Again

Only scattered feathers
That the wind will blow away
If not tomorrow
Then today

Solitude was bitter
But bitterness was sweeter
Than this constant heart's migraine.

Author Profile

Kaylie Rose is a poet by heart and has been writing in prose since the age of ten when her fifth-grade teacher read her poem 'The Pond' to her entire class. She has also published a poem entitled 'Shadow On the Snow' in a poetry collection called 'Circular Whispers'. She lives with her son and three cats in a small town in Pennsylvania

www.ingramcontent.com/pod-product-compliance
Lightning Source LLC
Chambersburg PA
CBHW070412200726
48294CB00003B/1171